ALFIE

A FRIEND FOR LIFE

Also by the Author:

Alfie Far From Home – Coming soon!

For adult readers:

Alfie the Doorstep Cat

A Cat Called Alfie

Alfie's Kitten – Coming soon!

ALFIE
A FRIEND FOR LIFE

Cat In Trouble

RACHEL WELLS

HarperCollins *Children's Books*

First published in Great Britain by HarperCollins *Children's Books* 2016
HarperCollins *Children's Books* is a division of HarperCollins*Publishers* Ltd,
HarperCollins *Publishers*,
1 London Bridge Street,
London SE1 9GF

The HarperCollins *Children's Books* website address is
www.harpercollins.co.uk

1

Text © Rachel Wells 2016
Illustrations © Katy May Green 2016
Rachel Wells and Katy May Green assert the moral right to be identified as
the author and illustrator of this work.

ISBN 978-0-00-817208-4

Printed and bound in England by
Clays Ltd, St Ives plc

MIX
Paper from
responsible sources
FSC www.fsc.org **FSC™ C007454**

For my wonderful son, Xavier

Chapter One

Sitting under a bush, I stared at a van, which two big men were unloading furniture from. I was about to move closer when my best cat friend, Tiger, appeared.

'Alfie?' she said.

I flicked my tail up in greeting. 'Hello,

Tiger. Look, people moving in!' I was always excited by the sight of a removal van. You see, I am a doorstep cat. I visit more than one house and have lots of humans who think they own me. Of course, in reality I own them. But that is why removal vans have such a fascination for me. They mean new people, and new people need a cat.

I might make some new friends to play with and if I'm lucky they might even give me yummy food – pilchards are my favourite.

'Alfie, this isn't even our street, what are you doing here?' Tiger was annoyed by my doorstep antics. She had one family and she liked it that way. But I loved my families – I had three altogether: one main home and two others, but I always say you can never have enough humans. Or pilchards for that matter.

'It's only round the corner.' We were in the street next to mine, Edgar Road. 'I'm in trouble again,' I admitted.

'What did you do?' Tiger raised her whiskers.

'Why do you always assume it's my fault?'

'Because it usually is, Alfie.'

I raised my whiskers back at her in protest, but Tiger was right. 'It's to do with baby Summer – she isn't sleeping. She cries all the time. She sounds like you when someone steps on your tail.'

'Thanks Alfie.' She glared at me with her yellow eyes. 'Anyway, what has that got to do with you being in trouble?' She licked her brightly striped fur; it was clear why she had been named Tiger.

'I'm just trying to explain,' I huffed. 'I'm tired, and Claire and Jonathan are tired and grumpy.'

'And?'

'And at breakfast I was half-asleep so I stumbled into my food bowl. My paws got covered in food so I panicked and somehow managed to tread it all into the carpet.' I shuddered as I remembered how Claire and Jonathan, my normally lovely humans, had shouted at me and called me a 'pest'.

'So, they're cross?' Tiger asked, sounding sorry for me.

'Yes, so I decided to lie low for a while. And in doing so I've found a new family, just to spend a bit of time with.' I wasn't planning on running away or anything like that.

'I guess that's fine but I *know* you. Don't get too involved with them – don't poke your whiskers into their business,' Tiger said. I nuzzled her neck.

'Don't be silly, of course I won't,' I replied. Honestly, Tiger didn't need to worry so much. After all what could possibly go wrong?

I made my way to the new house. It was easy to sneak in – the door was wide open, and the men were still carrying furniture so no one noticed me. I found myself in a big room that opened onto a kitchen.

There was a tall, thin man unpacking a

lot of fruit onto the kitchen counter. There were more bananas, oranges and apples than I had ever seen. He seemed to be taking a great deal of care, polishing them and putting them down very gently. It seemed a little strange.

'Dear, could you leave that and help me?' a woman shouted. She was shorter than the man, with big glasses and hair like a bird's nest with lots of pencils sticking out of it.

'But my fruit,' the man replied.

'I am sure it'll be fine for a few minutes, Dear,' she said. 'We need to organise the furniture.'

I watched as the two removal men moved

sofas, tables and chairs while the woman kept changing her mind about where they should put things. They huffed and puffed as they went backwards and forwards a lot.

'But Mrs Clover, you said it'd be fine here!' they complained as they lifted the biggest sofa I'd ever seen.

'Yes, well I thought it was, but it just doesn't look right. Please can you put it by the window? Yes, that'll do nicely. What do you think dear?'

The man, I assumed Mr Clover, was staring at an apple, which was painted a bright yellow.

'What? Oh yes, oh lovely.' He obviously wasn't paying attention but Mrs Clover seemed happy.

There was a little girl in the corner of the room. She had a book hiding her face and seemed not to notice the commotion. I thought about approaching her, but then a boy entered the room. He looked a bit scruffy: his clothes were far from neat, he had a cheeky round face with freckles dotted across his nose and messy hair. He was carrying a box, out of which he kept dropping things. As some of them rolled towards me, I saw they were stones. He looked a bit lost. He tried to get his parents' attention but his voice wasn't heard in the commotion.

Mrs Clover was giving orders; Mr Clover was looking lovingly at his yellow apple and the girl had her head in her book. With a thump, the boy suddenly dropped his box

and stones flew out across the floor.

'AHHHHH!' Mr Clover shouted. Both the boy and I looked on in horror as Mr Clover skidded on a stone, slipped along the wooden floor and ended up with his head in a plant pot.

'Stanley, what have you done?' Mrs Clover screeched. She sounded cross. Stanley was red-faced as he started scooping his stones up. 'You are such a calamity,' she bellowed.

'Sorry, sorry but it's my special stone collection,' the boy protested, sadly.

'My head, it's stuck, it's stuck!' Mr Clover shouted, his voice muffled by the pot. As he tried to pull it off, he banged into the wall.

'I think it was an accident,' the girl said, in a quiet voice, but no one took any notice.

'Stanley you need to be more careful,' Mrs Clover yelled, as Mr Clover's head was freed by the removal men.

'Sorry,' Stanley mumbled again. I moved

towards him; he definitely needed a friend.

'YOWL!' I slipped on a stray stone and fell over. My bottom ached, my tail hurt and I was lying on my back with my legs in the air.

'Oh gosh, it's a cat!' Stanley exclaimed, scooping me up and giving me a much needed cuddle.

'Miaow,' I said.

'Wow, how did you get in here? Do you live here? Who are you?' He seemed very pleased to see me.

I purred.

'Look, Mum, Dad, Viola! Look it's a cat! A CAT!' he shouted.

Still, no one seemed to hear him. Mr Clover had dropped his yellow apple during the plant pot incident and one of the removal men had stepped on it. Mr Clover was looking upset as he cradled the squishy mess. I thought he might have had tears in his eyes. The removal men were lifting a piano as Mrs Clover was telling them how precious it was and Viola was at her side. No one noticed Stanley or a lone cat.

'No one ever listens to me.' Stanley looked very upset as he took me and his stone collection out of the room.

We went upstairs, sat on his bed and he read my name tag.

'Alfie, that's a good name for a cat.'

I miaowed in agreement.

'We had to move here from the country.
I miss it.' He looked sad as he stroked me,
still clutching his stones. I purred in support.
'My sister, Viola – she's a podigy.'

I tipped my head questioningly; I'd never heard of a 'podigy'.

'It means she is very good at music. She has to go to the best music school so the whole family had to come here. She's eleven and I'm only eight so I don't matter. I miss my old home. And Viola is so good all the time. She never gets into trouble. I always do.'

I miaowed excitedly – Stanley and I were the same!

'I don't mean it, but I can be a bit clumsy. Mum calls me Calamity Stan. Anyway, I'm glad you're here. Even if you don't live in our house you can visit, and we can be friends. Can't we?'

I nuzzled into Stanley. Yes we would be very good friends, I could feel it in my fur. I miaowed and jumped off the bed; it was time for me to leave.

'You will come back, won't you?' Stanley said.

I miaowed again. You bet I would.

Chapter Two

When I returned to the Clover's house the next day, I made my way under the fence and into the back garden. The kitchen door was open so I just walked in. Mr Clover was sitting at the table, painting the outside of the apples in rainbow colours. I wanted to know why he needed to paint fruit but I couldn't ask, being a cat. Mrs Clover was talking on the phone and cooking lunch at the same time. I wondered, fleetingly, if I would get any but it didn't smell like fish, so it wouldn't matter too much if I didn't.

'I can make two new designs for plates by next week,' Mrs Clover was saying. There was a pause. 'Yes of course, matching bowls.' She was stirring something on the stove and talking. 'Oh no!' she shouted, dropping the phone.

'What is it dear?' Mr Clover asked without looking up.

'I've made custard instead of mushroom soup,' she said, scratching at her messy hair. 'I must have mixed up the packets.' She looked puzzled.

'Oh dear, dear,' Mr Clover replied.

I thought this might be the maddest house I had ever visited.

'Never mind, custard soup will be delicious for lunch, I am sure,' Mrs Clover decided.

I was suddenly glad I wasn't joining them.

Half an hour later, I was distracted by the most beautiful music I had ever heard.

Viola, the 'podigy' was playing her piano and I was impressed. I went over to her and hopped onto her lap. She stopped and scooped me up, giving me a lovely cuddle.

'What a cute cat,' she said.

I snuggled into her; she was pretty lovely herself. She was taller than Stanley, with the same colour hair and freckles, and she wore glasses like her mum, although her hair was much neater. As she stroked me, Stanley ran into the room like a whirlwind.

'Alfie!' he said, grabbing me from his sister. Viola looked a bit surprised; so did I. 'I have to show Alfie something,' Stanley said, carrying me off.

'You are my friend not hers, Alfie,' he said as he took me upstairs.

I miaowed. Of course I could be friends with everyone but I wasn't sure Stanley understood that. I glanced back at Viola who looked unhappy as she watched us go.

'Anyway I am going to show you where Mum works. We call it the Clay Room and we are absolutely *not* allowed to go in there.' He opened the door.

'YOWL!' I said in my loudest voice. If we were absolutely not allowed to go in there, maybe we shouldn't?

'Oh it's all right, Alfie, no one will ever know.' Stanley crept in and I followed him,

although I was sure that it was a bad idea;
I could feel it in my fur.

I had never seen a room like it before.
There were boxes everywhere, and I could
see that the ones that were open were full
of pots. A massive wheel was set up in the
centre of the room.

'My mum is a very famous pottery maker,'
said Stanley. 'She designs things and then
a big factory makes loads of them to sell.'
I purred in understanding. 'My Dad, he's an
artist. You've probably seen him with funny
coloured fruit – that's what he paints. He
sells it to a gallery and they seem to like it.'
He sighed. 'They are both so busy, and for

me, moving here, not having any friends – well it's not so much fun at the moment.' He sounded troubled.

'Miaow,' I replied.

'Dad's not as successful as mum, but some people say he's a genius. We all think he's a bit bonkers. He's branching out into eggs next.'

I was lost for words.

I looked into the big container of clay and then at the potter's wheel. It was quite interesting.

'It's so cool isn't it?' Stanley said. I purred my agreement as Stanley picked me up. 'Come and see the clay,' he said as he walked towards a large bucket. 'Ahhh!' Stanley shouted, narrowly avoiding bumping into a large pot which was next to the clay. He wobbled and I felt myself slipping.

'YELP!' he dropped me and I landed in the bucket of clay. It was wet and sticky, not at all how I thought it would be. I panicked. I couldn't move – I miaowed, yelped and yowled.

'Oh Alfie, sorry, sorry, don't worry, I'll help you,' Stanley shouted, trying to free me from the clay. Finally, I was out but we were both covered in the sticky stuff; it was all over my fur and paws. So much for no one knowing we were here.

'You look like a clay cat!' Stanley laughed.

I wasn't amused. Oh boy, we were going to

be in so much trouble! We had no choice

but to go downstairs. I shuddered as we left

a trail of clay behind us; it reminded me of

home and the cat food incident.

We both stood in the doorway. Mr and Mrs Clover just looked at us.

'Heavens above!' Mr Clover said, dropping an orange. I could see where Stanley got his clumsiness from.

'Stanley what have you done now?' Mrs Clover asked.

'Sorry,' Stanley said. 'Alfie wanted to see where you worked and well, he sort of fell into a box of clay and it left a huge mess on the carpets.'

I stood as close to Stanley as I could, trembling with fear.

'I don't believe this; we've only been here five minutes and already you've ruined the carpets!' Mrs Clover bawled.

'But Mum,' Viola started saying. 'You said you hated the carpets, remember? You said they would be the first things to go.'

I looked at Stanley, who was still staring at the floor.

'Well, OK, yes that is true but still… That is no excuse for you breaking the rules and you two definitely need a bath.' She turned to us. I wasn't happy with that, I hated water of any kind – baths, ponds, even puddles. What had we done?

'I know,' Viola said, in her timid voice. 'It's so hot, shall we get the hosepipe?'

'Great idea,' Mr Clover boomed. For

the first time, he seemed to be looking at something other than his fruit.

'OK, I suppose so. Children, put your bathing suits on,' Mrs Clover ordered. 'Alfie, stay where you are. Don't move.'

I wasn't sure I could; I was stuck to the floor.

Viola and Stanley shrieked with laughter as Mr Clover swung the hosepipe around and they ran through the water. Tentatively, Mrs Clover removed the clay from my fur and paws, as I tried hard to avoid getting too wet.

'Well, you are back to normal. I assume grey is your normal colour?' Mrs Clover said

as she finished. I miaowed. I was grey but in some lights I had a blue tint to my coat.

'Well, this is a fun activity,' Mr Clover chuckled and the children cheered.

I wasn't having very much fun, not being a fan of water, but seeing my new friends happy was almost worth getting wet for. The phone rang and Mrs Clover rushed indoors. She emerged a few minutes later. 'Viola, quickly get dried. You're seeing your new piano teacher this afternoon, I can't believe we nearly forgot. Dear, can you sort out Stanley? She said, turning to Mr Clover. 'Viola get dressed and practise.'

'But Mum—' Viola groaned.

'Chop chop, hurry hurry.' Mrs Clover wrapped Viola in a towel and took her inside. Mr Clover put the hosepipe away and Stanley and I stood, dripping, alone on the lawn.

'It's always the way – we start having fun and she has to ruin it,' Stanley huffed.

'Miaow?' Did he mean his mum?

'Viola. It's always about Viola and her piano. No one even notices me half the time. More than half really.'

I wanted to tell him that Viola had been enjoying herself, too. She hadn't wanted to go in.

'Come on Stanley, get yourself dried and

dressed,' Mr Clover said, going inside.

I knew that I had a job to do. Stanley was sad; Viola seemed a bit miserable, too. Mr and Mrs Clover were distracted but in the garden they had all enjoyed themselves. I knew my mission here was to remind them that they could have fun together.

A little while later, I found Tiger chasing butterflies at the end of Edgar Road.

'Hey,' I said.

'What's wrong, Alfie?' she asked. She could always read my moods.

'I've just left the Clover's. It's not a happy place. Stanley gets into trouble because he's bored and the grown-ups are obsessed with work.'

'Oh, Alfie, not another family to worry about?'

'I went there to get away from my problems at home, not find more, but I want to help them.'

'You always do,' Tiger stated as she jumped at a butterfly, missed and fell head-first into a bush. I couldn't help but laugh as she brushed leaves off.

'It'll all be all right. I'll think of something.'

'Well, in the meantime, do you fancy going to the park?' Tiger asked.

'If we can roll around in the flower beds

and chase flies, it might cheer me up.' I was worried, but a bit of fun never hurt a cat.

'Come on then, Alfie, I'll race you there.'

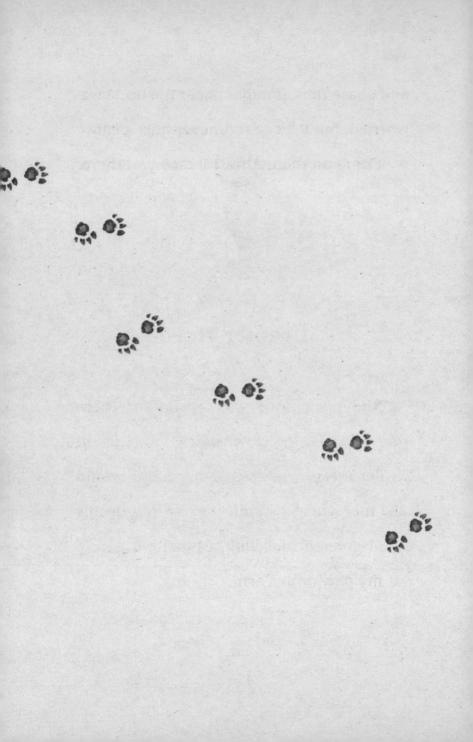

Chapter Three

The back door was open, but there was no one downstairs. I ran up to Stanley's room as fast as my paws would take me, where I found him, sitting on his bed. I greeted him with a purr and gently put my paw on his arm.

'Alfie, I'm glad you're here,' he said. I miaowed. 'I was supposed to have an adventure with Dad today. But then Mum had to work in the Clay Room, so Dad had to take Viola to her piano lesson. And I had to stay here.' He folded his arms across his chest and made a face. I tried to tell Stanley that we could have an adventure – after all I am quite good at them – but he didn't seem to understand.

'My parents prefer her to me. It's clear.' He stamped his foot before sitting down next to me again. 'They moved here for her and I miss our old home. I had lots of friends and lots of adventures. Dad and I would go and pick fruit together but now he goes to the boring old greengrocer instead and I don't even get to go with him.'

I knew that Stanley's parents did love him. After all, no matter how cross my families were with me they still loved me and I loved them. But how could I tell Stanley this?

'All I want to do is be an adventurer, but how can I when I can't even practise?'

I had an idea. I saw a pair of binoculars nearby and I went up to them. Gently, I nudged them, as if to say I could help him, but somehow I managed to get myself tangled in the strap. Part of it was round my neck and part round my legs. The more I tried to untangle myself, the more stuck I became.

'MIAOW, MIAOW,' I said as loudly as I could. That got Stanley's attention.

'Oh wow, good idea, Alfie. We can have adventures together!'

Finally! It took him a while to untangle me, so binoculars were now added to the list of things I needed to avoid.

'One minute.' I sat still and watched as Stanley rushed around the room collecting stuff. Then, he put a hat with flaps on me; I tried to swipe them away with my paw but they just flopped back over my ears. Next, he

wrapped a scarf around my neck. 'It might
be summer, Alfie, but when we explore the
North Pole it'll be cold.'

I didn't know what to say so I sat still
and let Stanley carry on. He started taking
photos; he was so excited. I didn't actually
like being dressed up; I mean what cat does?

But Stanley was happy as he snapped away with his camera.

'You are now Alfie the Adventure Cat and we are going to have so much fun. We can find fossils, build dens, dive for treasure. Oh I know – we can discover a species of animal never found before!'

I had no idea how we were going to do all those things, but I kept quiet. It was worth it to see Stanley happy. He pulled out a notebook and pen and started making notes. He also drew some pictures that were very good. His plans seemed extremely ambitious but I couldn't help feeling a bit excited. I quite fancied being

an adventure cat, even if I didn't know what
it involved.

While Stanley was busy drawing up plans
for our first mission, I thought I would go
and see what else was going on in the house.
As I walked past the next room, I spotted
Viola returning from her piano lesson. She
looked down in the dumps as she sat on her
bed, so I jumped up and nestled into
her. She started stroking me gently and I
purred.

'Oh look at you, in your hat and scarf,
I bet you've been having loads of fun with
Stanley?' She sounded sad.

I miaowed in agreement.

'You do look a little bit warm though, Alfie. Shall I help you take those off?'

I miaowed even louder to say what a good idea this was and Viola carefully removed my adventure outfit.

'I wish Stan would play with me more,' she said. Her voice was so much quieter than Stanley's. 'I miss being friends with him and I miss my old home.' She paused to wipe a tear from her cheek. 'I know we had to move so I could go to music school but it's a lot of pressure. I love playing the piano, I really do, and I like it here a bit, but at the same time I'm scared about my new school.'

She had tears in her eyes. I wished she
would talk to Stanley – they were both
feeling the same. I brushed my tail on her
wet cheek and she smiled as it tickled
her. 'I'm glad you're here,' she said quietly.

'LUNCH,' Mrs Clover's voice boomed. Viola jumped up, dried her cheeks with her sleeve and ran downstairs with Stanley on her heels. I followed them into the kitchen where four bowls of pasta were laid on the table. I was glad it wasn't custard soup again, although there was still no sign of any pilchards.

'Oh Alfie, I have something for you too,' Mrs Clover said, putting a bowl with some tuna on the floor. I licked my lips and miaowed my thanks. Today was looking up.

The family were quiet as they ate, as if they were all lost in their own thoughts. I started eating but kept one eye on them.

Stanley was staring at his food as he shovelled it in; Viola played with hers. Mrs Clover was humming an unknown tune and Mr Clover was eating with one hand while holding an egg with the other. It was a bit odd, as I had come to know the Clovers could be.

'What's for pudding?' Stanley asked when he'd finished.

'Um, go and help yourself to some fruit,' Mrs Clover replied. Stanley got up from the table, picked an apple off the counter and took a bite. As he walked back to the table with it, I sat at his feet.

'AHHHH!' Mr Clover screamed. Everyone

looked up and Stanley dropped his apple in surprise. It landed on my head.

'YELP!' I cried.

'That was my apple!' Mr Clover shouted.

'But Mum said to get some fruit, and it was on the side.' Stanley sounded upset.

'Yes, dear, I did,' Mrs Clover agreed.

'And Dad, it looks like a normal apple,' Viola added.

I rubbed my head with my paw. Who knew apples could be so heavy?

'Well, it wasn't a normal apple. It was a special apple that I was planning on painting later,' Mr Clover moaned.

I had an idea. I went to sit on a big pile of

empty bags from the greengrocer's.

'Miaow,' I said loudly.

'Oh, look at Alfie! I know, why don't we all go to the local greengrocer's and help you choose some even better apples?' Viola suggested, pointing at me.

'Better apples?' Mr Clover repeated.

'Great idea!' Stanley sounded excited.

'Please, let's go,' Viola said.

'All right, it'll be a bit like old times.' Mr Clover finally had a smile on his face, as did the rest of the family. I grinned as well.

Everyone went to get ready for their outing and I waited by the door. As I left, I realised that I still had a lot of work to do.

I had to bring the family together and help them see how much they needed each other. Because it was clear that they *did* need each other and they all really needed me.

I left them at the corner and made my way home. Tiger was lying in the sun at the end of our road.

'Hey Tiger,' I said.

She opened her eyes. 'Alfie, you're back early today.'

'The family have gone out together. Only to get fruit, but it's a start.'

'So, you think that whatever it is you're doing is working?' Tiger rolled onto her stomach and looked at me.

'It's early days but I'm a confident cat.'

'As long as you know what you're doing.'

'Oh Tiger, how could you say that? I always know what I'm doing.'

Tiger flicked her tail at me as if to say 'yeah right'. 'How about we forget the humans for a bit and go and tease some dogs?'

She didn't need to ask me twice.

Chapter Four

I wandered around the house, but there was no sign of Stanley. I went to see Viola who was playing the piano as usual. She stopped when I jumped onto the stool next to her and she made a fuss of me.

'Hi Alfie, it's nice to see you.' She had

such lovely manners.

'Miaow,' I said; it was nice to see her, too.

'I'm afraid Stanley's in trouble again. He pretended he was skydiving earlier, jumping off the sofa. It was funny but Dad got cross because he was being loud and I was supposed to be practising my scales.'

I rubbed up against her. This wasn't what I had hoped to find after yesterday.

'He's been sent outside. I didn't want him to go. He was having so much fun, I wished I could have joined in. I mean Stanley doesn't seem to like me very much sometimes but I wish he did. We used to play

62

together in our old house, I miss that—'

'Viola, I can't hear the piano,' Mrs Clover shouted. Viola sighed and I felt bad. I wished she could confide in me more. She looked downcast as she started playing again so I decided to cheer her up. I jumped onto the keys and tried to play with her. She looked surprised, then she giggled and we played together, although I found it quite hard. The keys were unsteady and it was difficult to balance.

'Plink, plonk,' I played but suddenly my leg slipped, and I crashed onto the keys.

BANG! My bottom hurt. To be safer, I sat on the keys and tickled Viola with my tail; she giggled.

'What on earth is going on?' Mrs Clover asked, coming into the room.

'Sorry Mum,' Viola said. 'Alfie was playing the piano.'

Yikes, I was in trouble now. Would I get banished, too? But Mrs Clover just laughed.

'Oh you silly cat! And by the way you are no Mozart,' she said, laughing even harder. I purred with joy as they both laughed, although

I had no idea who or what Mozart was.

'What's so funny?' Mr Clover asked as he walked in with Stanley in tow. 'Dear, I said Stanley could come back in; I think he's spent enough time in the shed.'

'Fine, but Stanley, and Alfie actually, can you please stay out of mischief? If Viola doesn't practise she'll be in trouble.'

'OK, Mum,' Stanley said, grumpily. 'Come on, Alfie. Let's go upstairs.'

I felt bad about leaving Viola, but I followed my friend upstairs and into his room.

'I'm so fed up; she's always telling me off, and Viola gets all their attention. Sometimes I think they don't even want me in the house.

Oh well, at least I like the shed. I mean, I can't tell them that – they think being sent outside is a punishment, but I think the shed is going to be my headquarters. I've put my special stones in it, as well as photos and plans that I've drawn up.'

'Purrr,' I replied.

'And I've just had the most brilliant idea. Adventurers have to work both on dry land and under water so I thought I could practise today.'

'YOWL!' No, not water.

'I shall get ready and you can be my assistant. Basically, that means you just have to be with me.'

I felt relieved; I wasn't planning on being involved in any underwater missions, thank you very much.

Stanley raced around, putting on a pair of swimming trunks, a pair of funny looking rubber things on his feet and goggles over his eyes.

'Right, so I have trunks, flippers and goggles. All I need now is my stopwatch and the bath.' The flippers made him walk in a funny way. A bit like an upright frog.

He filled the bath and got in. I sat beside the bath, a safe distance from the water. Stanley took a deep breath and started his stopwatch. Then, with the arm holding the stopwatch sticking out of the bath, he went under. After a while, his head emerged from the water; he spluttered as he looked at his stopwatch.

'Not bad,' he said. 'But I need to do better.' He took a deep breath and went under again.

I waited. And waited. I moved a little closer to the bath but I couldn't see anything. I was pretty sure that no one, apart from fish, could spend so much time underwater. I panicked. What if something happened to him? I jumped up onto the side of the tub. Stanley was very still under the water and I didn't know what to do. I peered over the

side, about to reach out with one paw, when
suddenly he sat upright, knocking my paw,
and me into the bath.

S<small>PLASH</small>!
'Y<small>OWL</small>!' I screamed.

'Alfie!' Stanley grabbed me quickly and
lifted me out.

I was horrified as I shook the water out of my fur. 'Alfie,' Stanley repeated.

I was soaked and, in a panic, I ran downstairs. I was yelping as I jumped up onto the kitchen counter, skidded and went headfirst into a basket of eggs. They all flew off the counter and smashed. I sat there, soaking wet and covered in yolk.

'My eggs!' Mr Clover screamed.

'What on earth?' Mrs Clover exclaimed.

Viola said, 'Stanley!' They all turned to where Stanley stood in the doorway, dripping wet, still wearing his flippers, goggles and trunks.

'I am guessing you can explain this?'

Mrs Clover bellowed.

'My eggs!' Mr Clover repeated. I licked some of the egg off my fur; it wasn't bad.

'Well, you see, I was practising being underwater—' Stanley started.

'Underwater?' Mrs Clover looked horrified.

'Yes, in the bath. And Alfie came and sat on the side of the tub; I seem to have accidentally knocked him in. It's well known that cats don't like water. Then he screeched loudly, and ran down here. I just came to see if he was all right.'

'My eggs!'

It seemed Mr Clover was very fond of those eggs.

'I don't even know where to start. Stanley, you know you are not allowed to have baths on your own and as for being underwater – what if something had happened? Do you really think Alfie would have been able to rescue you, you silly boy?' Mrs Clover yelled.

Stanley looked at everyone and at me. I would have found a way to rescue him, but I didn't know how to tell them that.

'No one would be bothered if anything happened to me anyway,' Stanley shouted. 'You don't care about me at all.' He stamped his flipper and tried to run off, but he could only manage a wobbly walk with his legs out straight. It would have been funny if he wasn't so upset.

Viola looked distraught; Mrs Clover looked shocked and Mr Clover was still staring at the broken eggs.

'What a worry that boy is.' Mrs Clover looked upset.

'But maybe he just thinks you're cross,' Viola said, reasonably.

'Viola, can you try to get Alfie cleaned up?' Mrs Clover asked, ignoring her. 'And Dear?' she said to her husband.

'My eggs,' he repeated. He really was unreasonably attached to them.

'For goodness sake, forget the eggs and

come and speak to your son. He needs to learn to be more careful, and you need to help me.' Mr Clover looked up. 'And, besides, how many times have you been told not to put all your eggs in one basket?'

That evening, having recovered at home with a long nap, I went to look for Tiger.

'Oh dear, someone looks a bit down in the dumps,' she said as she joined me in her back garden.

'It's just all gone wrong at the Clovers. I've never known a family like it.'

'I warned you to leave well alone, but you never listen.' Tiger yawned. 'I'm a bit tired, but if you want we can go and look at the moon; it might cheer you up.'

'You're a good pal, Tiger.'

'Yes I am, and maybe if you weren't so intent on saving the world you'd remember that a bit more.'

We both sat and stared at the bright round moon and Tiger was right – it did cheer me up.

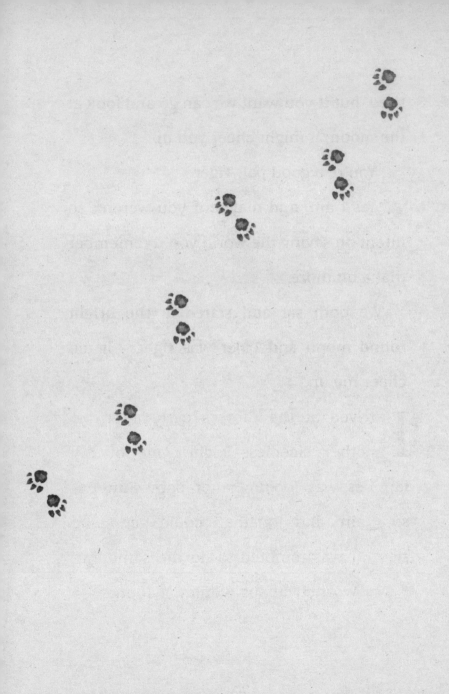

Chapter Five

I arrived at the Clovers early after yet another sleepless night. One of my families was looking after baby Summer so Claire and Jonathan could get some sleep. I was tempted to do the same, but I was worried about Stanley. I found the whole of the Clover family in the kitchen, finishing breakfast. Mr Clover was eating an egg – so it was all right for him to eat them but not for me to accidentally break them.

Mrs Clover seemed cheerful, Viola was smiling but Stanley was quiet.

'Right, so Dear, do you remember what I said?' Mrs Clover asked.

'What exactly was that?' Mr Clover replied.

'Tut. Please, listen and you too, Stanley,' she said. Stanley made a face. 'I have to take Viola to her new school. Dear, you're in charge of making sure your son doesn't get into trouble. Stanley you are in charge of staying out of trouble. You too, Alfie,' she said, noticing me. 'Come along, Viola. We don't want to be late.' Mrs Clover went to put her shoes on and I followed her so I could say goodbye.

'Mum.' Viola pointed at Mrs Clover's shoes. 'Your shoes don't match.' One was red and the other green.

'Pah, never mind, no one looks at feet.'

I miaowed. I did.

'So I have to keep Stanley out of trouble?' Mr Clover said coming to the front door.

'Yes, you should be able to manage that, shouldn't you?' Mrs Clover replied.

Mr Clover looked as if he absolutely couldn't.

As Stanley and his Dad cleared up the breakfast things, I managed to get myself some leftover egg; I had acquired quite the taste for it.

'Right, Stan. I have to paint some fruit. I won't be long but can you occupy yourself for a while?'

'I usually do,' Stanley mumbled sadly.

I rubbed against his legs. I felt sorry for him – he only got his parents' attention when he was in trouble. It was the same with me at my house at the moment.

'Alfie, let's go to the garden,' he suggested, huffily.

'Miaow.' I followed him outside, but he didn't seem happy as he kicked at stones. I hadn't seen him this miserable before. I tried to encourage him to play with me. There was a frisbee on the ground which I nudged towards him.

'Oh, it's my frisbee,' Stanley said, throwing it. I jumped up to try to catch it, but it was way too high.

'Brilliant, Alfie, try again.' Stanley suddenly looked happier. I kept jumping for the frisbee, although it was very tiring and I didn't manage it.

'Try again,' Stanley shouted and threw it. I jumped but when I landed on all fours I saw the frisbee flying over the garden fence.

'Whoops,' Stanley said. I jumped up onto the fence and took a look. I was met by unfriendly snarling. The frisbee had landed next to a very big, very angry looking dog. I felt my fur stand on end.

Stanley dragged a garden chair over and stood on it to see over the fence. 'I'm guessing the dog won't throw it back so it's down to us, Alfie.'

Count me out, I thought.

'I've had a brilliant idea!' Stanley shouted running to the shed. He returned, carrying a long stick with string attached and a large hook on the end. 'Dad's fishing rod,' he told me as he climbed back on the chair, wobbling a bit. 'If I can hook the frisbee,

I can get it back. Any adventurer would do the same.' He looked pleased with himself as he flung his arms back and then forwards and I watched the line and hook flying through the air and...

CRASH! The rod had hit the greenhouse roof next door. The dog started barking. Two people – a lady and man – ran out of the house just as Mr Clover appeared.

'Stanley, what have you done?' he shrieked.

'But Dad—'

'I don't want to hear it, Stanley,' Mr Clover shouted. Stanley's shoulders slumped as he wandered off to the other end of the garden. 'I am so sorry,' Mr Clover said to the neighbours as he stood on the chair and surveyed the damage. 'So very sorry. I'll pay for the repairs to your greenhouse.'

'Oh, don't worry,' the man said, smiling kindly. 'We don't use it. We've been meaning to get rid of it actually.'

What a nice man, I thought, as the dog growled at me.

Mr Clover looked relieved. 'Are you sure?'

The neighbours nodded.

'Well, I must do something. I know, I'll give you a piece of my art. Wait there,' he said, running back into the house and emerging a few moments later. He climbed back on the chair and handed a red banana over the fence. The man looked at the women as Mr Clover smiled at them expectantly.

'Well, gosh, I mean, thank you,' the woman said.

The man stared at the banana looking puzzled.

'Oh you are most welcome, and thank you,' Mr Clover finished.

'I have to paint another banana,' Mr Clover told us as Stanley and I stood by the back door. 'Can you please stay out of trouble for five minutes?'

Mr Clover was still mumbling to himself

– something to do with kids being a pain in his bottom and fruit being far less trouble, as he headed back inside.

Stanley was still looking glum but then, all of a sudden, he seemed to perk up. 'Hey Alfie! I know how we can stay out of trouble and practise our adventuring: we can build a den.' He went to the shed, and came back with a pile of things. He then went inside and brought out some poles and a blanket.

'Purr,' I replied, although I didn't know what a den was.

'So, we have a blanket, two garden chairs, some chicken wire and some funny poles I found. All any adventurer needs for the perfect base camp for our missions.'

I followed Stanley as he set about building. I jumped on one of the chairs as he stuck the chicken wire in-between them.

I wondered why it was called chicken wire, it looked nothing like a chicken.

'Off the chair, Alfie, or you'll end up lost under the blanket.'

I did what I was told. He put the poles into the ground and ended up balancing the blanket over the whole thing. I crawled into the opening. It was big enough for me to live in, not that I would.

'Wow,' Stanley said as he joined me. 'This is the best den ever.' I was caught up in his excitement. 'Right, so Adventure Cat, our next mission is to find fossils. We need to dig for them.' He put a hat with a big brim on me and picked up a bucket and spade. The hat slipped over my eyes and I had to use my paws to push it back. I wished I didn't have to wear it but I didn't want to upset Stanley. I slowly followed him round the garden. As he dug, Stanley sifted through the mud and put his findings into the bucket. Most of it looked like rubbish to me but he seemed pleased when he found a coin and a plastic toy.

'You see, Alfie, being an Adventurer is very serious so we need all the practice we can get. Come on, help me dig.'

'Miaow.' I tried, but digging wasn't one of my best skills. I found it almost impossible and my paws got covered in mud. Stanley, though, managed to make quite a mess of the lawn.

'Back to base camp,' he announced finally. I followed him as he emptied his bucket to examine his findings. 'A ring-pull, a five pence piece, a plastic aeroplane and four worms,' he said. 'No fossils so far. Oh well, we must not give up but now we must rest.'

I sat on his lap, eyeing up the worms that he'd put in my hat suspiciously. They were wriggly and without fur so I didn't trust them.

'STANLEY CLOVER!' Mrs Clover's voice boomed angrily. We looked at each other and poked our heads out of the den. We came face to feet with Mrs Clover, Mr Clover and Viola. Mrs Clover pulled the blanket off and shrieked. She and Viola had just arrived home.

'What are you doing with my special poles?' she asked. She was red-faced and her glasses fell off, she was so angry.

'What special poles?' Mr Clover asked.
Mrs Clover grabbed a stick and the den collapsed.

'My den!' Stanley cried out.

'These, Stanley,' Mrs Clover hissed, 'are poles from the rain forest of Papua New Guinea in South America and I was using them for a very important piece of artwork.'

She looked so red, I thought her head might explode.

'Oh dear, dear,' Mr Clover said, calmly. 'Look they'll be fine.' He went to collect the rest of the poles. 'Just a bit of mud that we can dust off,' he added reasonably. Mrs Clover examined them and then slowly returned to her normal colour.

'You see, nothing was really wrong, was it?' Viola said.

'You were supposed to be watching him,' Mrs Clover pointed at Mr Clover.

'Ah, well you see, I was but I had to go inside and paint a banana. I gave my other one as a peace-offering to next door.'

'Next door? I don't understand.' Mrs Clover looked confused. I wanted to cover my eyes with my paws. Now we were in real trouble.

'Stanley had an accident with a fishing rod and next door's greenhouse,' Mr Clover explained.

'I can't even leave you two for a couple of hours.' Mrs Clover's face was so red again it looked as if it might explode.

'I'm sorry, but I was trying to be an Adventurer. I wish I could go to South America,' Stanley said sadly.

'You won't be going anywhere other than your room, young man,' Mrs Clover shouted.

'What on earth happened to the lawn?' Mr Clover suddenly asked, noticing the holes. Stanley hung his head. Mrs Clover's jaw dropped open and I quickly sat down to hide my paws which were still a bit muddy.

'Oh no, we must have moles,' Viola said quickly.

'Moles?' Mr Clover asked.

'In London?' Mrs Clover added. 'Do you get moles in London?' I looked at Stanley who was staring at his sister, open-mouthed.

'Oh yes, I read about it, it's a real problem,' Viola said, as if she knew what she was talking about. I didn't think she did; I'd lived in London for all of my six cat years and never even seen one mole.

'Right, well I better go and look up how to get rid of them.' Mr Clover went into the house.

'And Stanley, you can repair the lawn before you go to your room,' Mrs Clover said. She was angrier than ever as she clutched her poles and marched inside.

Viola turned to Stanley who looked as if he was going to cry.

'Don't worry, Stan, I'll help,' she said quietly.

'Thank you for saying it was moles, Vi. I really didn't want to get into any more trouble.' Stanley smiled sadly at her.

'You're welcome,' Viola smiled back. As they filled in the holes, Viola tried to cheer Stanley up by making jokes and I sat watching. They really could be the best of friends, I thought, but they just needed a little bit of help. Luckily, I was here.

The lawn fixed, Stanley slunk upstairs to his room. I wasn't allowed to go with him. I felt bad and powerless as I sat in the kitchen, trying to think. Viola was now practising her piano; Mrs Clover was cleaning her rainforest poles and Mr Clover was making a display of his latest project: black apples. He was admiring them, looking very pleased with himself.

I knew then, even more clearly, exactly what I had to do. Viola and Stanley should be sticking together. So now, all that was left was for me to figure out exactly how to unite them.

Chapter Six

It wasn't a very happy house as I appeared at the Clovers. Stanley was in his room, lying on his bed. He didn't even cheer up when I arrived. Viola was alone in her room, reading a book and looking sad. She didn't make even half as much of a fuss of me as she usually did. I was so determined to come up with a plan to bring Stanley and Viola together but they seemed further apart than ever, and I hadn't even got a proper idea yet. I noticed that Mrs Clover was shut in the Clay Room. Did no one in this family spend time with each other? The doorbell rang and so I went downstairs. Mr Clover was holding a pink egg as he opened the door.

'Hello?' he said.

'I'm Mr Ivory the piano tuner,' the man standing on the doorstep said. He was large and had a big bag with him.

'Oh, I'd quite forgotten about you,'

Mr Clover said. 'Do come in.'

I followed them to the piano.

'Wow, that is a beautiful piano,' Mr Ivory looked excited.

'Well, yes, but it's no egg,' Mr Clover replied. The piano tuner gave him a funny look.

I stayed with Mr Ivory. It was quite interesting watching him work, although I had no idea what he was doing. At the same time, I started to formulate a plan to bring Stanley and Viola together. It was the piano that took up most of Viola's time and her parents seemed to be preoccupied with it, too. Stanley felt neglected and too upset to see that Viola could help him, if only he would let her. As Mr Ivory tinkered with this and that, making some very odd noises along the way – the piano not him – I realised that it could be part of my plan. Perhaps I could learn to play a tune. Viola and Stanley would be so happy, or they would find it so funny, that it would bring them together.

I am not just a pretty cat, you know.

When Mr Ivory had finished, he went to find Mr Clover. I jumped up to start practising but the top of the piano was still open and I climbed up to have a look. It was bumpy but warm as I lay down for a minute. I was tired after all the thinking I'd been doing. I yawned and closed my eyes, just for a short cat nap...

I opened my eyes. It was pitch black. I blinked. I couldn't see a thing.

'YOWL!' I realised I was inside the piano; the lid was closed. I tried to nudge it with my paw but it wouldn't open. I was trapped. In a piano! What on earth was I going to do? I miaowed, yowled and yelped as loudly as I could and just as I was beginning to think I would be here forever, I heard voices.

'But he has to be here,' I heard Stanley

say. He sounded distraught.

'But we've looked everywhere, Stan,' Viola replied. 'Maybe we should get Mum and Dad?'

'As if they care.'

'Oh Stan, they do, I know they seem a bit distracted…'

'Except when they're shouting at me. Face it, Vi, they love you better.'

'Oh Stan, don't say that.' I heard her protest as she sat on the stool, and hit some keys.

'OW!' that hurt.

'He wouldn't have gone without saying goodbye,' Stanley said; they hadn't heard me.

'Calm down, we'll keep looking,' Viola sniffed. 'Honestly, Stan, I'll help you, I want to help.'

'It's been horrible since we moved here,' Stanley said. 'Alfie is the only good thing about it.'

'I miss our old house, too,' Viola said.

'Do you?' he asked. I heard him sitting down and he bashed the keys.

'OW!'

'Yes, very much,' Viola said. 'Oh Stanley, I just want to be your friend.'

'Really?' Stanley sounded unsure.

'Of course, I love it when we play games together. It's so much fun.'

'It is fun, isn't it? Maybe we could do more, you know, like you could help with my adventures?' Stanley sounded uncertain.

'Yes, I'd really like that. Let's start by looking for Alfie together.' Viola sounded more cheerful.

'OK, I'm really worried, Vi,' Stanley added.

I took a deep breath and gave my loudest 'YOWL!', and quickly followed it up with another one.

'What was that?' Stanley asked.

'I think it came from inside the piano,' Viola replied. The piano lid slowly opened and I jumped out, straight into Viola's arms.

'Alfie, thank goodness!' Stanley said.
I purred my thanks as Stanley stroked me.
'Thanks Vi,' Stanley mumbled, and Viola
smiled. See, I knew they could be friends.
Viola moved towards Stanley and, still
holding me, she hugged her brother.

Mr and Mrs Clover walked in.

'Ah, there you are children. Is the piano all right, Viola?'

'Perfect,' she replied, giving Stanley a funny look. They both giggled.

I had done it; I had made them laugh, and they had made friends. I didn't even have to learn how to play the piano after all.

As I approached my house, I found Tiger sitting under a bush in my front garden.

'Hey,' I said, feeling proud.

'Why do you look like the cat who's got the cream?' Tiger asked. I licked my whiskers.

'Yum, I wish I did have cream.' Suddenly,

I remembered I was quite hungry. 'Well, if you must know, I have managed to solve all of the Clover children's problems.'

'Oh Alfie, here we go again,' Tiger said, rolling onto her back. She could be a very negative cat.

'No, honestly, it was genius. I knew I needed to get them to spend more time together and now they are going to. Alfie strikes again!'

Tiger looked at me as she swiped her paw at a passing fly. She missed then she rolled back and stood on all fours.

'I guess you are going to tell me about it, whether I like it or not?'

Of course I was. 'Well, it all began with a piano…'

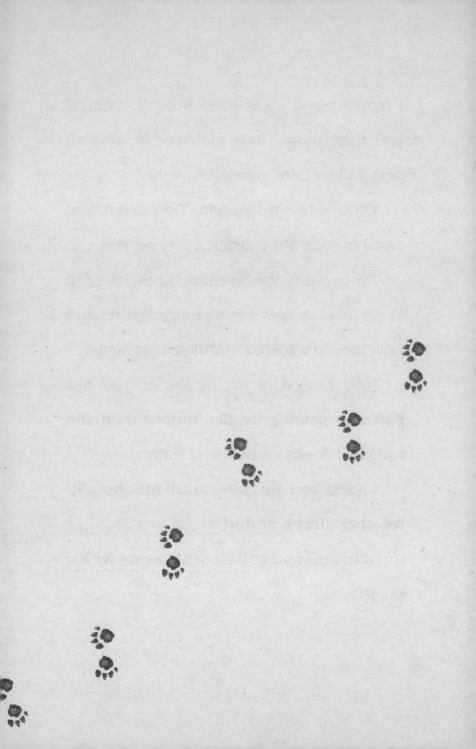

Chapter Seven

Stanley was sitting at the kitchen table with a box in front of him when I let myself in. I jumped up. It had wriggly worms in it. I backed off slightly; I still didn't trust them.

'Miaow.'

Stanley looked sad. 'Oh Alfie, hi, I was just looking at my worm collection. Every Adventurer needs a collection of wild animals.'

'Miaow!' He had me. He didn't need worms.

'You don't count Alfie, you're not wild.' I didn't know whether to be offended or not.

'Anyway, I am so totally bored today. I don't

know what to do. Mum and Dad have been spending all their time with Viola. She's playing them her new piece of music.' He looked at me. 'She was going to play with me, but they wouldn't let her.'

Oh dear. Poor Stanley. He had made friends with his sister but he was still upset by his parents. I had an idea. I jumped off the table and went through to the living room, knowing that Stanley would follow. He did. Viola was playing her new piece of music, her mum and dad were standing watching her. I approached with Stanley just behind me, clutching his box of worms.

'Bravo,' Mrs Clover clapped. She had

tears in her eyes.

'Viola, that was brilliant,' Mr Clover said.

'Such a talented girl,' Mrs Clover added.

Viola blushed. I could see Stanley getting angry.

'Look everyone, I've got a worm collection,' Stanley said, standing right behind his parents.

'What?' Mr Clover swung round and bumped into Stanley.

'Ahhh!' Stanley said, dropping his box.

'AHHHHHHH!' Viola screamed as worms landed in her lap. She jumped up then tripped over. 'Oww.' She landed on her bottom, her glasses flying across the air.

'Sorry,' Stanley said, scooping his worms up. I wasn't sure if he was apologising to Viola or the worms.

'Right, Stanley that is it,' his mother shouted. 'Worms do not belong in the house and look what you have done to your sister.'

'I'm fine, honestly, Mum,' Viola said. But everyone ignored her.

'You never pay any attention to me.' Stanley shouted.

'Well I am paying attention to you now, young man,' his mother said, waggling her finger at him. 'You will say sorry to Viola, and then you can go to your room and think about your behaviour.'

Stanley ran off.

'I just don't know what to do about him,' Mrs Clover said as I went to follow. 'No Alfie.' Mrs Clover picked me up before I reached the stairs. 'Stanley needs to learn to behave himself, so I am afraid you will have to leave today. Come back tomorrow.' She opened the front door and put me outside.

I hadn't done anything and I was being banished! I was beginning to understand why Stanley was so angry with his parents. I sat on the steps feeling cross, before deciding that I might as well go to the park. With any luck Tiger would be there. I started walking slowly, taking my time. The sun was beating down, birds were flying overhead, and I stopped to look at flowers. My good mood returned as I enjoyed my journey.

No sign of Tiger as I made my way to the flower bed. I was just about to dive under my favourite bush when…

'Yelp!' Stanley was right behind me. I knew children shouldn't be out without a grown up and although I was six cat years old, I didn't qualify.

'Hi Alfie,' Stanley looked very pleased with himself. He was wearing a big hat, had a pair of binoculars around his neck and was holding his compass.

'Miaow?'

'An Adventurer needs to be able to stalk without being detected. I decided to practise by following you.'

'Miaow?'

'Mum and Dad were so busy, they didn't see me sneaking out. They don't care anyway. Besides, you didn't notice me following you which means I'm very good at it.'

I knew we were going to be in big trouble for this. I tried to get Stanley to go back home by walking to the park exit but he wouldn't. He collected some leaves, and then he climbed up one of the smaller trees.

'Um, there is not much on the horizon,'

he said, looking through his binoculars. 'Ah, some rare species of plants.'

I had no idea what to do, so I just stayed with him. After what seemed like ages, he came down from the tree.

'I suppose I'd better go home; it's probably nearly tea time,' he said. Finally. I rewarded him by brushing my tail against his legs. 'Right, let's go.' He took out his compass. 'Oh dear, which way is home?' We stood at the park exit. I knew, so I miaowed but he didn't seem to hear me. He looked at his compass and started running round in circles. 'My compass is broken and now I am totally lost!' he shrieked as he started getting breathless. I tried to get his attention but he was spinning too much. 'Oh no, I am going to have to live in this park forever!' Stanley shouted. He was huffing and puffing, sweating and distressed.

'Miaow, miaow, miaow!' I screeched. Finally, he stood still. I started walking, hoping he would follow me and, still holding the 'broken' compass, he finally did. I led him home as quickly as my legs would allow.

'Wow, you really are an adventure cat,' he said, as we reached his front door.

We rang the doorbell, and although I didn't want to wait, I knew I couldn't abandon Stanley now. Mr Clover opened the door.

'Oh my goodness, there you are!' he said. Stanley hung his head.

'Where have you been?' Mrs Clover shrieked as soon as she saw him. Viola burst into tears.

'Sorry, but—'

'No, Stanley you have gone too far this time,' Mrs Clover interrupted. 'It's not safe for children to go wandering off; anything could have happened to you.' Mrs Clover was more upset than I had ever seen her.

'We were worried sick, Stanley,' Mr Clover shouted. 'Worried sick.'

I looked at Stanley who looked at his feet. He was bright red.

'You are to go straight to your room,' Mrs Clover started crying. 'And you are not to leave this house, not even to go in the garden.'

'Not fair.' Stanley threw his compass. It flew through the air and I could barely look as it smashed into one of Mrs Clover's pots.

'My new pot!' she screamed. Mrs Clover started to cry as Mr Clover hugged her and Viola.

Stanley looked at the three of them, huddled together and, without them noticing, he ran into the garden.

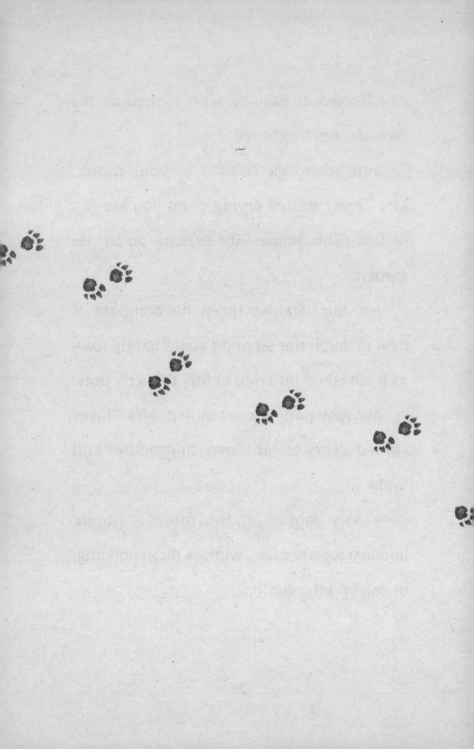

Chapter Eight

I needed to go home but first, I had to mend the Clover family. They were quite broken. I followed Stanley to the shed, where he sank down on the picnic blanket and sobbed. I went over to him and rubbed up against him, purring to let him know

I was there for him.

'Miaow.' Gently, I put my paw on his arm.

'I didn't mean to break the pot,' he said sadly. 'Now Mum and Dad will be crosser than ever with me. They might send me away.'

'Miaow.' Of course they wouldn't.

'They don't want me here.'

I looked around. My Adventure Cat photos and drawings were on the walls and his collections were laid out on shelves. He had made it very cosy here but I knew he needed to go back to the house.

'I am never going back to the house,' he said. So much for that.

I waited with him for ages but he wouldn't move. It was getting cold and even a little bit dark. We couldn't really stay here forever, could we? I knew I needed to act. When Stanley was calmer, I left him to get help. It was a job for more than just me.

'Where on earth can he be?' Mrs Clover was shrieking. I miaowed to tell them I knew, but they didn't seem to hear me.

'He can't have gone far, Dear, after all we locked the front door and he can't get out the back.'

'He can't have disappeared into thin air,' Mrs Clover said. They both looked worried as they talked about calling the police. I couldn't believe no one thought to check the shed.

'What are we going to do about him?' Mrs Clover asked.

'Maybe you just need to talk to him,' Viola said, sounding cross.

'What?' Her parents turned to look at her.

Viola sighed. 'We've just moved here. Stanley has no friends apart from Alfie.' I was moved by the mention. 'And you're so busy. He thinks it's all about me and the piano.'

They both looked at her in confusion. Sometimes humans can be a bit silly.

'So he keeps getting into trouble because we've moved?' Mr Clover scratched his head.

'It's not *just* that but basically, yes. And it's school holidays, so he's bored and you just shout at him. He thinks you love me more than you love him.' Viola had tears in her eyes.

'Nonsense,' Mrs Clover said. 'We love you both the same. Why on earth would he think that?'

'But we don't do anything together, do we? When was the last time Dad took Stanley out? Or you, Mum? Or the last time we did anything as a family?'

'Oh dear, dear,' Mr Clover said, looking guilty.

'I see, Viola. We've been so busy we've neglected him.' They both hung their heads in shame.

'We must find him,' Viola pushed.

I had never heard her sound so bossy and I liked it.

Mrs Clover organised a search of the house, but of course I knew where he was. I stood between Viola's legs and kept miaowing.

'What is it Alfie?' she asked. I nudged her leg and then I walked out into the garden. I turned back, yelped at her and she began to follow me.

'Oh Stanley there you are! Mum and dad are really worried,' she said, as I pushed open the shed door.

'No, they just want to shout at me,' Stanley huffed.

'Honestly, they aren't cross. They just

want to know you're safe.'

'They don't care. I'm rubbish at everything and they only love you,' Stanley said. 'They probably want to send me away.'

'They don't, Stan. I spoke to them and they realise they've been too caught up in their stuff. They're really sorry.'

'Are they?' Stanley looked hopeful.

Viola nodded. 'Hey, what's all this?' She looked at the pictures.

'Alfie the Adventure Cat,' Stanley replied quietly.

'You did all this?' Viola asked.

'Yes.' Stanley stood up. 'See, here are my photos of Alfie the Adventure cat, and over there are drawings of our missions,' he explained, pointing to a picture of the den and the dug-up lawn. 'And I've done descriptions and maps of ideas for new adventures.' Stan was animated as he showed Viola round the shed.

'Wow, Stan, it's brilliant!'

'Really?' Stanley asked.

'It really is. So amazing. I know it hasn't been easy moving here. I've been scared and Mum and Dad, well they are—'

'Always too busy for me unless they're shouting.'

'They only tell you off because they care. They wouldn't bother if they didn't.'

I miaowed. Viola was right.

'I suppose,' Stanley replied.

'And I thought we were friends now. I haven't got any friends here, either, you know.'

'Sorry Vi, but I was jealous. You never get into trouble.'

'But I don't mean to be like that. And I'm jealous of *you* – you know how to have fun much more than I do.'

'OK,' Stanley stood up. 'Let's make a pact: we'll try to be a bit more like each other – I'll get in less trouble and—'

'I'll get in more!' Viola giggled. 'Come on, let's go. Mum and Dad are far too silly to even think of looking for you in the shed, and they were talking about calling the police.'

Viola hugged Stanley and he hugged her back. I miaowed. This was exactly the outcome I wanted.

'Oh Stanley, we were so worried,' Mrs Clover said as she grabbed him, holding him so tight I wondered if he could breathe.

'I'm sorry that I keep doing things wrong,' Stanley said. He hung his head as I sat at his feet.

'Well, that is how we learn; I mean, you don't think I just painted a piece of fruit and that was that – no, I made plenty of mistakes,' Mr Clover said.

'Um, well anyway, we need to make more time for you – for both of you, but especially you, Stanley. So we are all going on a family holiday,' Mrs Clover announced.

'Hooray!' both Viola and Stanley replied.

'And we will start by making your favourite tea.'

'Sausages and chips?' Stanley was wide eyed.

'Whatever you want,' Mrs Clover added.

'As long as it's not custard soup,' Viola said and everyone laughed.

I knew my work here was done. For now.

Quietly, I let myself into my home through my cat-flap. It was late and I was tired after such an eventful day, hungry too.

'Oh Alfie,' Claire said as I walked into the kitchen. 'We were worried about you.' She scooped me up and cuddled me.

'I know we've been grumpy but we missed you, Alfie,' Jonathan added. I purred with happiness.

'And to show you how much we love you, we've got your favourite tea.' Claire rubbed my head.

'Pilchards,' both Claire and Jonathan said at the same time. I licked my lips and felt my whiskers quiver in anticipation.

This had turned out to be the best day ever.

Enjoyed this book?

Then follow Alfie's next adventure as he
accidentally goes on holiday...

For adult readers:

And coming soon... **ALFIE'S KITTEN**

THE *SUNDAY TIMES* BESTSELLER

ALFIE

A FRIEND FOR LIFE

Far from Home

RACHEL WELLS

Coming soon!